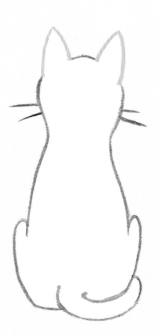

THE ASTRONAUT'S CAT

TOHBY RIDDLE

ALLEN&UNWIN

SYDNEY·MELBOURNE·AUCKLAND·LONDON

To everyone at St Canice's Primary, Katoomba – TR

All photographic images of the Moon were taken by astronauts of Project Apollo and are used courtesy of the United States' National Aeronautics and Space Administration (NASA).

Images of butterflies, bees, dragonflies, crickets, birds and fish, except those on pp26–27, are courtesy of the Wellcome Collection.

The typeface for this book is Futura Medium. After the author chose this font he discovered that Futura was the font used on the plaque left on the Moon by the astronauts of Apollo 11.

First published by Allen & Unwin in 2020

Allen & Unwin
83 Alexander Street
Crows Nest NSW 2065
Australia
Phone: (61 2) 8425 0100
Email: info@allenandunwin.com
Web: www.allenandunwin.com

A catalogue record for this book is available from the National Library of Australia

The paper in this book is FSC® certified. FSC® promotes environmentally responsible, socially beneficial and economically viable management of the world's forests.

ISBN 978 1 76052 494 4

For teaching resources, explore www.allenandunwin.com/resources/for-teachers

Illustrated using digitally assembled collage techniques, including pencil drawings, photographs, hand-drawn cut-outs from acrylic-paint or ink textures, and antique engravings or watercolours of flora and fauna.

Cover and text design by Tohby Riddle and Jo Hunt
Set in 19pt Futura Medium by Tohby Riddle and Jo Hunt
Printed in December 2019 in China by Everbest Printing Co., Ltd

10 9 8 7 6 5 4 3 2 1

The astronaut's cat
is an inside cat.
And she likes it like that.

Inside has air.
Outside doesn't.

Cat likes air.

Outside, there are only rocks and dust.
Cat isn't so keen on that.

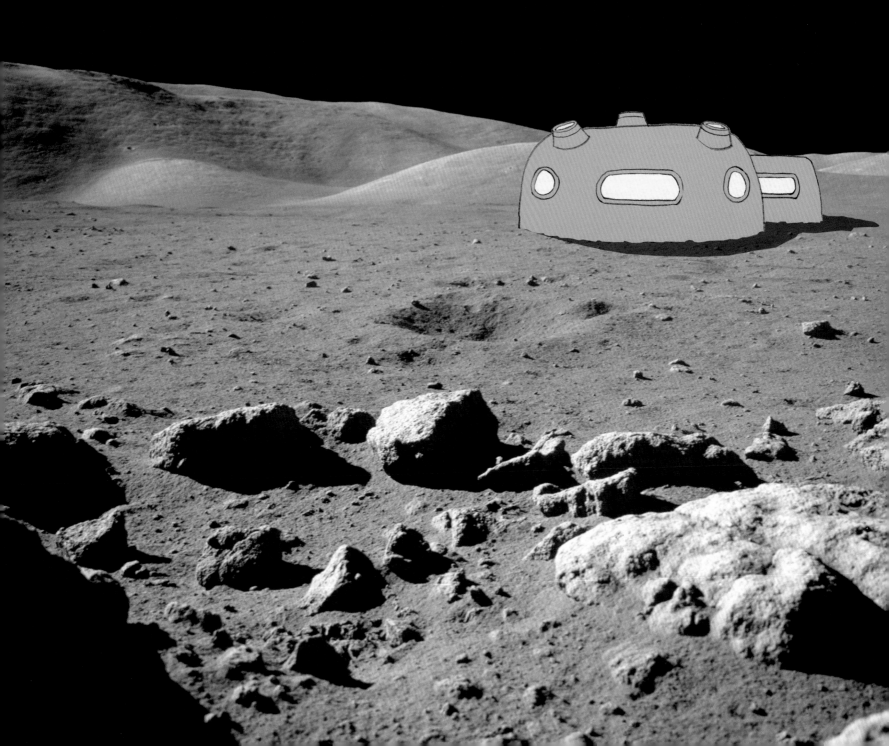

But Cat does like to look outside.
Outside looks amazing!

Inside, Cat has lots to do...

She plays with her ball.

She eats.

She sleeps.

She plays with her ball again...

Outside, it's so hot in the sun that
a bowl of water would quickly boil.
'Ouch!' thinks Cat.

But at night it's ten times colder
than a fridge freezer.
'Brrr!' thinks Cat.

Then there are tiny rocks

called micrometeoroids

whizzing around

at ten kilometres per second.

That troubles Cat.

And there's no sound. Cat likes sound.
The sound of the bell in her ball… The sound of Astronaut…

But outside still
looks amazing!

And in Cat's dreams,
she goes outside . . .

She leaps and pounces
further than she's ever
leapt or pounced.

She glides from silvery rock to silvery rock.

And she bounces in the fine grey dust
like she's lighter than a birthday balloon.

Then she dreams a blue ball
rising in the ink-black sky.

And in her dream she dreams...

She's on that big blue ball.
Everywhere there is colour and movement,
and a million million shapes and forms.

It's not too hot
and it's not
too cold,

and water flows
in rivers, and
pools in ponds.

And sweet air fills her full with a thousand scents,
and carries sounds that make music.

And there she is
an outside cat.

Then Cat wakes up from her dream...

She remembers that she's the astronaut's cat,
and she's an inside cat.

And that is that.